EGMONT

We bring stories to life

First published in Great Britain in 2007 by Dean,
an imprint of Egmont UK Limited
239 Kensington High Street, London W8 6SA

Thomas the Tank Engine & Friends™

A BRITT ALLCROFT COMPANY PRODUCTION

Based on The Railway Series by The Reverend W Awdry
Photographs © 2007 Gullane (Thomas) LLC. A HIT Entertainment Company

Thomas the Tank Engine & Friends and Thomas & Friends are trademarks of Gullane (Thomas) Limited.
Thomas the Tank Engine & Friends and Design is Reg. US. Pat. & Tm. Off.

HiT entertainment

ISBN 978 0 6035 6237 2
7 9 10 8 6
Printed in Singapore

Gordon Takes a Tumble

The Thomas TV Series

DEAN

Gordon was a very proud engine. In fact, he thought he was the brightest, shiniest engine of all!

Gordon loved it when his paintwork was admired, but his favourite thing was speeding up and down the tracks, taking passengers to their destinations.

One day, Gordon had to deliver passengers to the Docks.

Gordon smiled as the passengers admired his paintwork, but he wanted to leave the Docks as soon as possible, so he didn't get dirty.

Salty pulled up alongside Gordon.

"Careful of my paintwork!" Gordon cried.
"I don't want it to get all sooty!"

"What's wrong with being sooty?" Salty said.
"I've been pulling trucks all day."

"I never get dirty," said Gordon. "And I don't like
pulling trucks; it's not dignified!"

That night, a large shipment arrived at the Docks and was loaded into trucks.

"Henry, Thomas and Percy, you must go to the Docks tonight," said The Fat Controller. "You will be coupled to the trucks so you can move them in the morning. And Gordon, I want you to help, too."

"An important engine like me should not pull trucks!" Gordon said.

But he had no choice.

At the Docks, Gordon waited impatiently as the trucks were shunted into place.

"Why are you in such a hurry?" asked Thomas. "We're not leaving until the morning."

"I'm going to show Salty how a real engine pulls trucks!" said Gordon.

"Be careful, Gordon," called Salty. "Don't you know that pride comes before a fall?"

At dawn, Gordon rushed out of the Docks, leaving Salty far behind. He raced along the tracks saying, "Now, this is how you pull trucks!"

But Gordon didn't realize that the points were accidentally switched to the branch line. He was going so fast that he was through the junction before anyone could stop him.

"That's funny," he thought. "What am I doing on the branch line?"

"Oh, no!" cried the Signalman. "Express trains can't go this way!"

The old branch line was weak. There were signs all along it saying 'Go Slow', but Gordon ignored them. "I'm an express engine," he said. "I never go slow!"

So Gordon raced on even faster.

The branch line began to buckle under Gordon's weight. Suddenly, the bolts snapped and Gordon slid off the rails and fell down the hillside!

"Ooh! Help!" he cried, as he rolled down the grassy hill.

Gordon came to a stop in a ploughed field in front of a scarecrow. He felt very undignified.

"What will The Fat Controller say?" he thought.

He was soon to find out.

"Well, Gordon," said The Fat Controller when he arrived. "I hear you wanted to show Salty a thing or two! You've certainly done that. You've shown him how silly it is to ignore 'Go Slow' signs!"

"I'm very sorry, Sir," said Gordon.

Gordon had to stay in the field for a very long time. Finally, the breakdown train came out to rescue him.

Heavy chains were tied around Gordon.
The breakdown train carefully winched him back
on to the track. He then had to wait until the
trucks were rescued.

Gordon had learnt his lesson – he travelled slowly
along the branch line until he reached the next
junction box. Then he waited for the Signalman
to switch the signal so he could get back on to
the main track, where he belonged.

Gordon was quickly repaired and he was soon back at the Docks. He was very quiet though, because he thought everyone would make fun of him for rolling down the hillside.

"Don't worry, Gordon," said Thomas. "Everyone makes mistakes – even you!"

"Salty was right though," said James. "Pride does come before a fall!"

"Yes," said Gordon. "It comes before a fall down a hillside!"

And everyone laughed – even Gordon!